Turtlee in Paris

Written and illustrated by Paris Stankewich

Happy reading!
Paris
Stankewich

DEDICATION

Dedicated to my loving family and to my plush turtle,
Turtlee, who is the star of the story.

Once upon a time there lived a stuffed animal named Turtlee. Turtlee's dream was to travel the world.

Turtlee *especially* wanted to visit Paris, France. He'd heard there was a famous painting called Mona Lisa and a **giant** tower called the Eiffel Tower.

Luckily, the girl who took care of Turtlee also wanted to travel to Paris, France.

One day, the girl finally got tickets to go to Paris, France. Turtlee just couldn't wait! His dream would start becoming true by being taken to France.

The flight to France was very long. Turtlee didn't mind, he was having too much fun thinking about what they would do in Paris.

Turtlee looked around as he, the girl, and the girl's mother exited the elevator. They stepped into the street, looking at Notre Dame, a big church. Paris, France was amazing!

They went to their hotel and checked in. The girl placed Turtlee down on the table as she went to pet the cat. "Bonjour! Je m'appelle Isaac." The cat purred. "Hello, Isaac! I'm Turtlee." Turtlee told the cat.

Bonjour (bon-zhoor): Hello
Je m'appelle (zhuh-mah-pehll): My name is

The girl stood up and grabbed Turtlee. "Bye Isaac. See you soon." Turtlee said, waving, as they left the hotel. "Au revoir!" Isaac replied.

Au revoir (oh-rev-wa): bye

The girl, Turtlee, and the girl's mother walked to Notre Dame. Turtlee loved being carried through the streets of Paris. Even the air felt good against Turtlee's face.

After going into Notre Dame, they climbed the many stairs up one of Notre Dame's towers.

The view at the top was amazing. You could see almost every part of Paris. The girl set Turtlee down on the ledge and turned around to take out her camera.

Turtlee leaned over the edge to get a better look at the gargoyles. The girl turned towards Turtlee and her elbow bumped him off the ledge.

Turtlee fell down and down. He tried to grab on to something as he fell, but there was nothing to grab.

With a soft *thump,* Turtlee landed right on someone's big purple hat. Turtlee looked back up at Notre Dame as he was carried away in the big purple hat.

After a while, the woman with the big purple hat climbed onto the metro, which is an underground train.

By the time the woman got off the metro, Turtlee was completely lost. The woman's phone began to ring. The woman pulled out the phone and started talking in French.

Suddenly, the woman shook her head. Turtlee was thrown off the hat and onto the street. Turtlee looked around. The woman was the only person on the street, except for Turtlee.

Turtlee then saw something move behind a tree. "Hello?" Turtlee asked, "Is anyone there?" A cat came out from behind the tree.

"Isaac!" Turtlee said, surprised. "Bonjour! Is that you, Turtlee?" Isaac asked. Turtlee nodded. "I fell off Notre Dame and then was carried away. Now I'm lost." Turtlee said.

"Climb on my back, and I'll take you to the hotel."
Isaac told Turtlee. Turtlee smiled and climbed onto
Isaac's back.

As Isaac wound through the streets of Paris, Turtlee was thinking about the girl and the rest of the trip.

Isaac and Turtlee finally reached the hotel where the girl was staying.

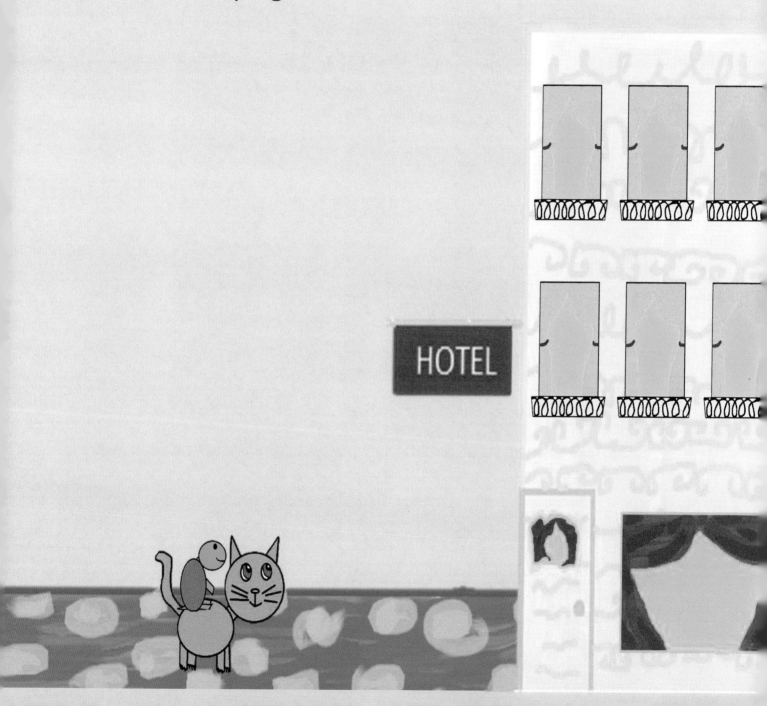

Isaac looked through the window. "Wait right here for the girl. She is probably going to come soon." Isaac said to Turtlee.

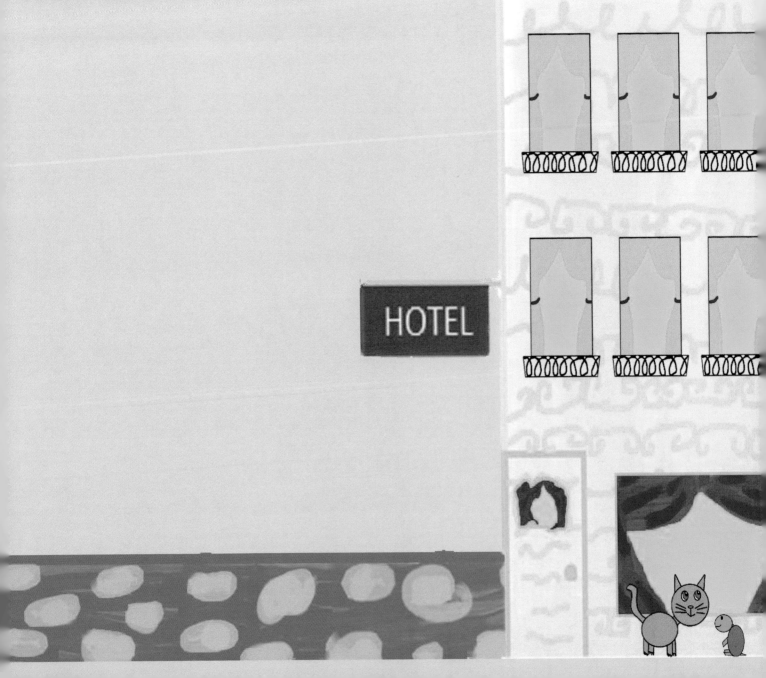

Turtlee waited as someone let Isaac into the hotel. Turtlee was looking at the ground when little hands picked him up.

"Turtlee!" The little girl said. Turtlee smiled as she gave him a big hug.

The Real Turtlee
in Paris

Paris Stankewich lives in North Carolina with her mother, father, and younger brother. She is currently in seventh grade and enjoys running, playing soccer, reading, writing, and hanging with her two Labrador Retrievers, Poppy and Gabby. This is the 1st book that she has written.

Made in the USA
Charleston, SC
06 December 2014